# NORMAN'S Gift

WRITTEN AND ILLUSTRATED BY
MICHELLE OLSON

Bellie Button Books

# For my best friend, husband, and fellow snorer

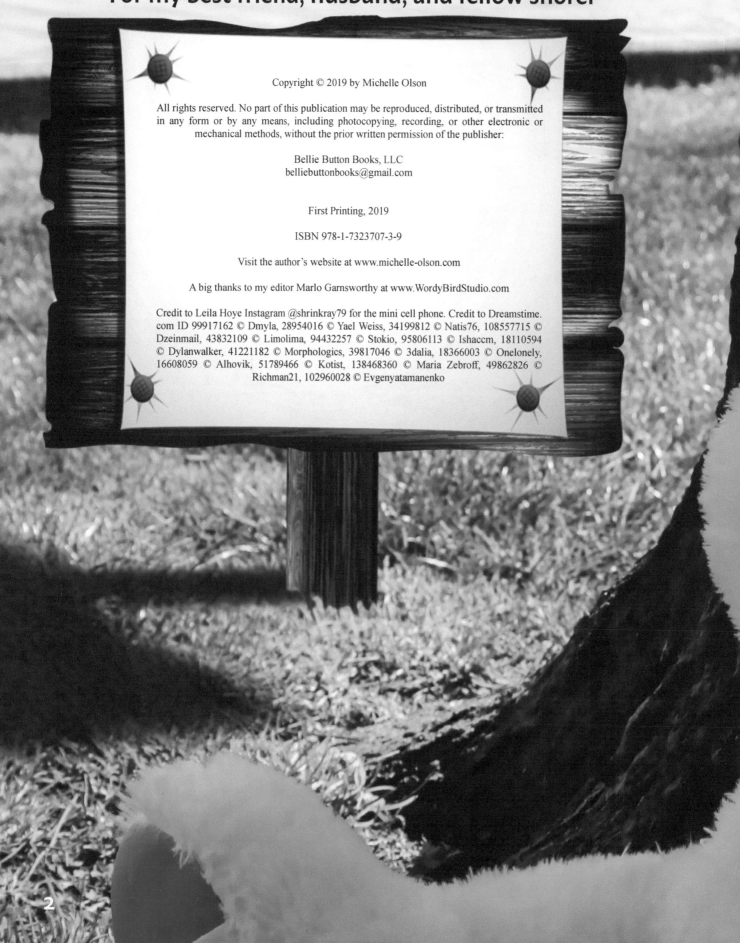

Bellie Button Books, LLC
belliebuttonbooks@gmail.com

First Printing, 2019

ISBN 978-1-7323707-3-9

Visit the author's website at www.michelle-olson.com

A big thanks to my editor Marlo Garnsworthy at www.WordyBirdStudio.com

Credit to Leila Hoye Instagram @shrinkray79 for the mini cell phone. Credit to Dreamstime.
com ID 99917162 © Dmyla, 28954016 © Yael Weiss, 34199812 © Natis76, 108557715 ©
Dzeinmail, 43832109 © Limolima, 94432257 © Stokio, 95806113 © Ishaccm, 18110594
© Dylanwalker, 41221182 © Morphologics, 39817046 © 3dalia, 18366003 © Onelonely,
16608059 © Alhovik, 51789466 © Kotist, 138468360 © Maria Zebroff, 49862826 ©
Richman21, 102960028 © Evgenyatamanenko

Norman the Button and Freddy Teddy were the best of friends. Neither was complete without the other.

The two friends were inseparable during the day. They giggled and joked until Norman was in stitches.

Knock-knock.
Who's there?
Macy.
Macy who?
We Macy your cousin today.

Knock-knock.
Who's there?
Sarah.
Sarah who?
Is Sarah do...

FUNNY JOKES

BY KAYLEE &
MCKENNA OLSON

4

At night, they stayed up late watching movies and eating snacks until Freddy was stuffed.

But when it was time
for bed, the two had to
part ways.

Freddy's snoring had become an unbearable problem for Norman. They both decided it was best if Norman slept in the playroom dollhouse.

One night, Norman awoke to Freddy's voice, so he got out of bed to investigate.

Norman gasped, "Christmas present! I don't have a Christmas present for Freddy. What am I going to do?"

Norman quietly snuck back to bed, but he couldn't fall asleep. He needed to think of an amazing gift for his best friend.

Norman was very tired when he rolled out of bed the next morning. But he was also very excited.

He had finally thought of the perfect gift.

WARNING: The currency used in this game is not real and is not intended for use in the real world. 11

Norman was shocked by how expensive cars were.
There was no way he could buy one for Freddy.

# Cell Phone

**by Applesauce**

★★★★ ▾      3 customer reviews  |  15 answered questions

## $1.00
### In Stock

**Add to Cart**

Free two-day shipping

Toy cell phone loaded with apps

Perfect size for dolls

Image not to scale

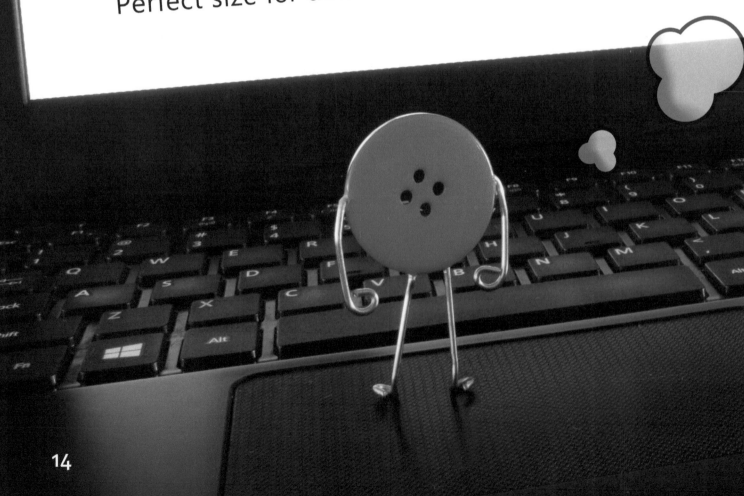

The next day, Norman had an even better gift idea.

"I guess this is why the phone was such a great deal," sighed Norman. "I used everything in my piggy bank. How can I buy something if I don't have any money?"

Norman decided if he couldn't buy Freddy a gift, he could make something instead. Like most bears, Freddy liked cakes made with honey best.

Norman figured three tiers would be just enough
to make his friend smile. Of course...

19

...Norman had never made a sandwich, let alone a cake. The moment he added the bacon, he knew something was very wrong.

"Ugh! I can't bake this," moaned Norman. "It looks disgusting!"

It was the night before Christmas, and Norman still had no gift for his friend. He had no money and wasn't good at baking. The only thing Norman felt he was really good at was knitting.

"I suppose I could knit Freddy a scarf," thought
Norman. "It has been very cold lately."

Norman was disappointed he couldn't give his friend the grand gift he had planned on getting.

24

"It's not going to be awesome like a car or a phone, but it *is* going to be the best scarf I can make," he concluded.

It was finally
Christmas morning,
and the two friends
exchanged gifts.

26

Norman was on pins and needles as he waited for Freddy to open his present.

When he saw the scarf, Freddy squealed.
"This is amazing! I love it, Norman," Freddy
exclaimed. "It's the best present I've ever gotten!"

28

Norman breathed a sigh of relief, and the two gave each other a hug. "You are my best friend Norman. Thank you so much for the scarf," said Freddy. "Now open your gift!"

"What do you think?" asked Freddy.

"Any gift that brings me closer to you
is the best gift ever," said Norman.

Please check out
my other books at

belliebuttonbooks.com

You can also download
a free teacher's guide
and coloring pages.

Norman the Button

CPSIA information can be obtained
at www.ICGtesting.com
Printed in the USA
LVHW071016130120
643357LV00003BA/3/P